This Makes Me Silly

DEALING WITH FEELINGS

by Courtney Carbone

illustrated by Hilli Kushnir

Random House 🏠 New York

Today I am going
to the zoo
with my family.

I cannot wait
to see the animals!

A tour guide
shows us around.
She pretends to talk
to some ducklings.

It makes me laugh.
My heart feels
warm and fuzzy
like their feathers.

We see elephants
playing in the water.
They have long trunks.

My brother and I act
like elephants, too.
My insides feel wiggly
like their trunks!

Next we see lions.
Our guide asks
if we know how to roar.

The answer is yes!
We all roar
as loud as we can.

Then we see the monkeys.
They make funny faces.
We make funny faces, too.

The monkeys get angry!
The tour guide tells us
not to tease them.

Soon it is time for lunch.

We have
a family picnic!
I feel as light
as a bird.

My brother eats
his banana
like a monkey.

I laugh so hard that water goes out my nose!

Dad helps us
to calm down.

We breathe slowly.
We count to ten.
The giggles go away.

After lunch,
we see a polar bear.
He is sleeping.

I put my hands
in the air like claws.
I feel big and strong
like a bear.

I pound on the glass
with my pretend paws.
The tour guide points
to a sign.

She tells me
loud noises can scare
some animals.

I stop to think.
Our guide is right.

It <u>is</u> scary to wake up
to loud noises.
I will be more careful.

The last stop of the day
is to see the penguins.
They are my favorite!

I waddle around
with our tour guide.
I thank her for
such a great day.

We pass a park
on the way out.
We stop to play.

I make lots
of funny faces.
My family does, too!

I feel like I am full of tiny bubbles about to burst!

My giggles are back.
But now I know
how to calm down
if I need to.

I close my eyes.
It is so much fun
to laugh, play, and
pretend.

What am I feeling?
I am feeling SILLY.

For Sara, who always makes me smile

—C.B.C.

*To Liam and Aya, who, along with me, turn being
SILLY into an art form*

—H.K.

Text copyright © 2018 by Courtney Carbone
Cover art and interior illustrations copyright © 2018 by Hilli Kushnir

All rights reserved. Published in the United States by Random House Children's Books, a division of Penguin Random House LLC, New York. Originally published by Rodale Kids, an imprint of Random House Children's Books, a division of Penguin Random House LLC, New York, in 2018.

Step into Reading, Random House, and the Random House colophon are registered trademarks of Penguin Random House LLC.

Visit us on the Web!
rhcbooks.com

Educators and librarians, for a variety of teaching tools, visit us at
RHTeachersLibrarians.com

The Library of Congress has cataloged the hardcover edition of this work as follows:
ISBN 978-0-593-56484-4 (trade) — ISBN 978-0-593-56485-1 (lib. bdg.) —
ISBN 978-0-593-56486-8 (ebook)

Printed in the United States of America
10 9 8 7 6 5 4 3 2

This book has been officially leveled by using the F&P Text Level Gradient™ Leveling System.

Mousella The City Chinchilla

By: Jessica Sweeney

MOUSELLA THE CITY
CHINCHILLA

Printed in the United States

ISBN 978-0-615-89291-7

A portion of the profits from the sale of this book will be donated to chinchilla rescues.

I dedicate this book to The Mouse, the Smart Girl, and the Sweet Man.

My name is Mousella.

I'm a chinchilla who lives in the city.

Actually, I live in a cage, in a
house, in the city.

I have a family of humans.

They take care of me and give me hay, pellets, and water every day.

They let me out of my cage at least once a day, so I can run around and play.

I'm an exotic pet.

Exotic means I'm unique and unusual, and my humans must take extra special care of me.

They have to keep the temperature in my home cool or I could overheat, which would be very bad for me.

I have soft warm fur because my native land is in the Andes Mountains in Peru where the temperature is cool.

My humans have done a lot of things to
keep the temperature cool enough for me.

Last summer we lived in an apartment that was hot.

My humans had to buy a special box that blew cold air into the living room.

Sometimes it was still too hot, even with the special box. Then they would have to freeze cans of food and put them all around my cage.

Now we live in a house that stays cool all the time, and my humans don't have to worry about me anymore.

My humans have a lot of visitors. They have friends and family over for dinner and get-togethers.

Their visitors always gather around my cage because most humans have never played with a chinchilla.

Humans are fascinated by me.

I am fascinated by humans.

I sleep in a little house most of the day.

Sometimes I peek my head out of my house when I hear things.

I can look around from a special hole in the top of my house and see who's coming and going.

I am called nocturnal because I sleep during the day and am awake at night.

My humans can't play with me all night because they sleep, so they leave PBS on the big black box for me to watch.

My favorite shows are cartoons and the exercise lady.

Sometimes I watch the big black box for hours, especially if my favorite shows are playing.

One of my favorite things is my daily treat.

I get 1 or 2 rose hips every day.

My humans used to give me raisins, but then they discovered that too many raisins are not good for my gentle digestive system.

Now my humans are trained to give me rose hips.

I get a dust bath 3 times a week.

I take baths in dust instead of water because my fur is not supposed to get wet.

My humans buy a special soft dust, and then they put the dust in a small container.

I love to jump in the container and roll around.

My humans give me willow sticks, which I chew to keep my teeth from growing too long.

I also like to dress up and wear funny little hats.

Sometimes I sit in my wheel with my funny hats and chew my willow sticks.

My humans call me The Big Mouse, or Mousie, or Cute Mouse. They are all my pet names.

Sometimes my favorite human, who takes care of me the most, will hold me so I can snuggle with her.

I love my humans.

My humans love me.

My name is Mousella, and I'm a chinchilla who lives in the city.

Mousella The City Chichilla was inspired by our pet chinchilla who is a fascinating creature.

After much research on the proper care of chinchillas, we have concluded that these special animals require a great deal of time and resources.

A portion of the profits from the sale of this book will be donated to chinchilla rescues.

To view pictures of Mousella and learn more about chinchillas, visit: www.citychinchilla.com

CPSIA information can be obtained
at www.ICGtesting.com
Printed in the USA
LVIC06n2106011113
359380LV00005B/44